The Kid Detective Cracks the Case

Solve Yourself Short Story Mysteries Book for Kids

Alice Elton

TABLE OF CONTENTS

YOUR FREE GIFTS

As a way of saying thanks for your purchase, I'm offering these books Inspiring Short Stories of Fascinating Animals and Basel Kid Detective Riddle and Puzzle Books for FREE to my readers.

To get instant access just go to:

https://springloftpublishing.com/free-gifts

Inside these books, you'll get:

- More entertaining short stories with powerful life lessons.
- Riddles and Puzzle book you can exercise your brain too.
- And more fun for the whole family!

If you want more inspiring stories and a good mind-twister, make sure to grab these freebies.

MESSAGE TO THE YOUNG DETECTIVES

Step aside Sherlock. Basel is in the building! Welcome to "Basel The Kid Detective Cracks The Case: Solve Yourself Short Story Mysteries Book For Kids" where you get to join the world's greatest detective, well, at least in Basel's mind he is, as he finds himself in the middle of intriguing and wild mysteries.

Basel is an average kid, but there was one thing he was better at than anyone his age. He loved solving mysteries. At first, he found mysteries in the smallest of things, that frankly, weren't so mysterious to begin with. That was until his first case came to his doorstep, and that too in a funny way. Our "greatest detective in the world" was suspected of theft. Now, it was a matter of honor. He had to clear his name.

We've compiled a collection of Basel's very first cases so you can take the journey with him. Together, you and Basel will navigate through the twists and turns of each case. Along with Basel's logic and your observation, analytical, and interpretation skills, you two will certainly be able to get down to the bottom of these mysteries. So, come along for the ride, and remember, "The game is afoot!" -Sherlock Holmes (Goodreads, 2021)

If you plan to learn more about how a detective solves different cases, don't forget to go through the Detective's Manual in the back of the book. It has been specially written with the help of Basel himself to train you in the best way possible.

Are you ready to join Basel on an adventure that will have you laughing, thinking, and scratching your head all at the same time?

Let's get solving!

THE LOST ASHTRAY

"The world is full of obvious things which nobody by any chance ever observes."

Sherlock Holmes, The Hound of Baskerville (PinkMonkey, 2019)

He had just finished his breakfast and was on his way back to his room when Basel passed the living room. He saw Grandma standing like a statue, looking at the glass cabinet that held all of her most precious decorations.

"Good morning, Grandma." Basel greeted.

"It's missing." His grandma mumbled.

That was when Basel finally saw what it was. "Mom's first-ever handmade ceramic ashtray is missing!" Basel immediately understood. "She gave it to you as a gift, didn't she?"

"Yes, she did, but where'd it go?" Grandma's voice was sarcastic as she turned to face him.

Grandma didn't like Basel most of the time because he never followed instructions and always did what was on his mind. Although he did usually end up getting into trouble.

"No, no, no," Basel immediately raised his hands and shook his head. "I didn't do anything!"

Grandma narrowed her eyes; she had just opened her mouth to say something when…

"Two days, just give me two days," Basel bargained. "I'll bring the real culprit to you."

***

"It is clear that the theft took place in the morning after the cleaning lady left the house. Otherwise, she would have informed you," Basel explained. "The cleaning lady left at 9 am, and you entered the room around 10 am. So, that's when the crime took place."

"These are our two main suspects," Basel pointed at two handmade drawings taped to the back of his room door.

Grandma simply rolled her eyes. "Why is your mom a suspect?"

"Mom had just given me breakfast," Basel explained, pushing his chocolate brown curls back from his forehead. "And right after that, she had suspiciously disappeared. Mom was in such a hurry to leave even though she had told me last night she had no plans for today."

"And what explanation do you have for the neighbor's daughter?" Grandma snorted.

Basel turned to face the last drawing. "*Alice...*" He mumbled, narrowing his eyes.

Basel never liked that girl. She was always hatching plans to get him in trouble.

"Alice had come in the morning to deliver cookies," he said aloud. "I don't think her intentions were so innocent. She'd do anything to get me into a sticky situation."

"So, how do we find out which one of them took the ashtray?" Grandma inquired

***

"Found it!" Basel cried out loud.

Basel and Grandma were back in the living room looking for clues.

"Found what?" Grandma asked excitedly.

Basel handed the magnifying glass to Grandma and pointed to the cabinet's glass door. "Look!"

"Oh my," Grandma gasped. "That's a fingerprint and quite the big one! But how are you so sure it's the thief's fingerprint?" Grandma asked. "Our cleaning lady could have left it."

"If she had opened the cabinet, then the racks and all the decorations would be clean too," Basel explained as he took the fingerprint using a piece of clear tape. "But there's still dust on the cabinet's shelf. This means it could only have been the thief who touched the inside of the glass door."

"Oh, you're smart," Grandma admitted, making Basel smirk. "But wait a second," she said, the magnifying glass still in her hand. "There is something else here."

Using the magnifying glass, Grandma picked up a long curly brown hair.

***

"This fingerprint is of thc thief's left thumb," Basel explained as he showed a section on fingerprints in the Detectives Manual to Grandma and pointed at the fingerprint they had found on the cabinet.

“So now we need to get fingerprints of both suspects to find out which one of them stole the ashtray,” Grandma concluded.

Their first target was Basel’s mom. The next day they woke up early and prepared a lovely breakfast for her.

Finding the right moment, Basel pretended to slip as he returned from washing his own plate. He ended up knocking over the fork his mom had just placed on her plate.

“Sorry, I’ll get it!” Basel quickly bent down before his mom could.

“Be careful honey,” His mom advised as she tucked her straight long brown hair behind her ear.

He realized he had also knocked down Grandma’s fork, but he hoped she’d forgive him for the mistake. After all, they had bonded over the theft, or at least he hoped.

Basel carefully picked up both the forks as Grandma offered his mom a new one. His mission was complete.

Then it was Alice’s turn. Later that day, Grandma invited her over to help arrange her fancy dinner plates.

"Basel, lovely little Alice is here to help us out too," Grandma announced cheerfully.

Basel tried to smile as best as he could, but it was hard to be nice to Alice. Basel, however, got a little distracted when he noted Alice, too, had straight brown hair.

"Honey, why don't you bring those two plates to me," Grandma requested, pointing at the plates on the counter. That finally brought Basel's attention back to the main issue.

The two of them watched as Alice picked up both plates in each of her small hands. With that, they had their second fingerprint in no time.

***

"None of them match the thief's fingerprint!" Grandma protested. "And they both have straight hair!"

Once Alice left, Basel and Grandma ran back to his room to get the fingerprint. Yet, it seemed all their plans were for nothing.

"How is this possible?" Basel muttered to himself.

"You lied to me the entire time, didn't you?" Grandma was furious.

"No!" Basel protested. "I must have made a mistake, but where?" He ran a hand through his brown hair in frustration.

Grandma was just about to storm out of the room when a cheer from Basel stopped her.

"Ah, I've been so senseless!" Basel cried. He looked up at Grandma with twinkling eyes. "I know who the thief is."

What did Basel do wrong during the investigation? Who is the real thief? Do you think you can find her? It's all in there. You can do it!

If you think you've cracked the case, go to the solution on the next page.

SOLUTION

THE LOST ASHTRAY

“What do you mean?” Grandma questioned suspiciously. She didn’t believe Basel was being honest with her.

“You remember how while knocking Mom’s fork on the floor, I’d knocked off yours too?” Basel asked.

“Yes, so?”

“That’s the thing. I confused your fork with Mom’s,” Basel told her excitedly. “That fingerprint is not Mom’s but yours. And since we didn’t make any mistakes with the other two fingerprints, it’s obviously Mom who took the ashtray!”

“I think there’s another thing we completely missed out too.” Basel continued. “It should’ve been clear that Alice didn’t do anything from the time we found the fingerprint on the cabinet.”

“What do you mean?” Grandma asked.

“Look at their sizes!” Basel laughed. “The thief’s fingerprint was a size too big to have been Alice’s.”

“And we kept on going about how both have straight hair, but one of them doesn’t!” Basel said, pointing at his curly hair. “Mom has natural curly brown hair like mine. She straightens it every day!”

***

“My Goodness, Mom, I never *stole* the ashtray.” Basel’s mom protested as he and Grandma confronted her. “I… I just broke it.”

“You what?!” Grandma said in alarm.

“I saw how you still had the ashtray I’d made for you and wanted to take a look at it.” Basel’s mom explained. “My hands were wet since I’d come from the kitchen and ended up dropping it. I knew you’d probably get mad, so I didn’t say anything. When I talked with you last night, you were normal, so I figured you were still unaware and I decided not to tell you. I had asked for a favor from an old friend to loan their workshop to me yesterday.”

She turned around to rummage through her bag and took out the brand-new ashtray, "I know it's not the same, but..." she ended her sentence with a sheepish shrug.

"So, that's where you had been all day?" Basel asked rhetorically. "You were making a new ashtray for Grandma."

His mom nodded at his words and pushed the new ashtray further into Grandma's hands.

"Oh, honey," Grandma's words were caught in her throat as she took hold of the delicate ashtray, "You shouldn't have done this, but anything you make is valuable to me." With that, she drew her daughter in for a long hug.

"Hey, how did you guys even know I broke the ashtray?" Basel's mom suddenly asked as she pulled away from Grandma.

"We have our ways," Basel simply smirked and winked at his grandma.

His heart soared as Grandma returned his wink with a smile of her own. I guess he advanced to her good books now as well.

SNIFFING FOR LIES

"You have to calmly dissect and scrutinize everything. Dig up the truth as rationally as you can."

Heinrich Lunge, 'Monster'
(Roychoudhury, 2021, para. 24)

"I think Mom read it."

Basel looked up from the video game he was playing in surprise. His sister Misty stood there, red in the face.

"Read what?" Basel asked in confusion.

It seemed Misty hadn't heard a single word. She nervously chewed on the skin of her thumb as she rocked on the balls of her feet.

Basel set his phone aside and walked up to his sister. "What's wrong, Misty? What did Mom read?"

That finally broke the spell. "Oh Gosh," Misty gasped. "I think Mom read my diary!"

Her words confused Basel even more. "Why would she?"

"Why wouldn't she?!" Misty said in a panicked voice. "She has always been curious about what I write in Ms. Cuddles...."

"Ms. Cuddles?" Basel laughed at the name Misty had given to her private diary.

"Not the topic," Misty frowned. "Anyway, where was I?

Ah, yes, Mom. She has tried so many times to catch me unaware so she can read it."

"I still don't think she did it," Basel shook his head. "But why are you so worked up even if she did?"

Misty blushed as she opened her mouth to speak when Basel raised his hands.

"Or no, I don't think I want to know." Basel made a dirty face. "Like I said, it can't be Mom. It must be someone else, but who?"

"I forgot to lock my diary before I went to take a bath. Fifteen minutes later, when I came back, it was lying open on the floor," Misty explained.

"It's only me, you, Mom, Dad, and our maid in the house," Basel counted on his fingers.

"It's certainly not you. Otherwise, you wouldn't be this calm had you read it." Misty responded.

Basel frowned and mumbled in a low voice, "Now I am curious to know what you write in there."

"That leaves Mom, Dad, and the maid." Misty continued.

"Well then, there's only one way to find out - we ask them," Basel said, stepping out into the hallway.

He was immediately hit by the subtle fragrance of the new lavender floor cleaner in the hallway. And then the smell of pancakes which made his stomach grumble.

"Let's go to Mom first," He announced, licking his lips.

They found her in the kitchen, setting the table for breakfast. Their mouths watered at the sight of chocolate pancakes, a treat they only got on Sundays.

"Good morning, darlings. You're here early," Their mom said as she saw the two of them.

"We just couldn't resist the smell of your amazing pancakes," Basel told her.

"Mom, where were you like half an hour ago?" Misty asked bluntly, impatient as always.

Their mom laughed at that, "I thought you were smarter than this. Where else would I be but in the kitchen?"

"She's gone crazy," Basel laughed awkwardly as he pulled his sister away.

As they made their way to the backyard, Basel chastised Misty over her blunt interrogation skills.

"Just let me do the talking, okay?" He whispered as the two of them drew closer to their father, who was busy watering his beloved flower bed.

"Morning Dad!" Basel and Misty greeted out loud.

"Good morning kids!" Dad smiled.

"It's one hot day, isn't it? Basel said, rubbing a leaf between his fingers.

"Sure is," Their dad replied. "I just came back from the store and bought a shade of cloth for my babies. The sun has been roasting the plants these past few days."

"Yeah, they need some protection," Basel nodded. "You better hurry up though. Breakfast will be ready soon."

He then excused himself and went back to the house, Misty trailing behind him.

"You made it look easy," Misty admitted, to which Basel simply smirked.

As they entered the living room, they saw their maid Hannah dusting.

"Morning Hannah," The siblings greeted.

"Morning," She replied, looking up as she was cleaning the legs of the coffee table.

"You must be tired from all this dusting." Basel sympathized. "You look like you need to take a break."

"I'm fine kids, thank you!" Hannah said awkwardly as she folded her arms across her chest. "Th...This is the first place I've cleaned all day." She said with a little stutter. " Umm… before that, I went outside to get the mail. Yeah, that's where I went."

"Misty, Basel, breakfast is ready!" Their mom called at that moment.

"We'll get going then," Misty said, leaving Hannah to her work.

As soon as they stepped into the kitchen, Basel passed his sister a clever smile. "I know who read your diary."

How did Basel conclude who the culprit was?
Can you find him/her out as well?
The clues are all in there.

If you think you've cracked the case, go to the solution on the next page.

SOLUTION

SNIFFING FOR LIES

"It's Sunday," Basel said excitedly.

It took a second before things finally clicked for Hannah too. "Of course!" She exclaimed. "No mail ever comes on a Sunday."

Basel nodded at that, "Correct! Hannah lied to us. She's the one who read your diary. She also said the living room was the first place she cleaned, yet, the floors outside our rooms smelled like lavender. Hannah cleaned them this morning too."

"She must have entered your room to tidy it up as well but was instead captured by your diary. When she heard you coming, she ran away." Misty concluded.

"Did you also note the way she spoke?" Basel pointed out. "Hannah had folded her arms across her chest. In psychology, a posture like that shows that a person is trying to protect themselves. I read something about it in the Detectives Manual. Why would Hannah feel there's something she needed to protect herself from if she'd done nothing wrong."

"Hannah..." Misty muttered as she shot imaginary lasers in the direction of the lounge.

"Told you it wasn't Mom," Basel said triumphantly. "Now I get to have two of your pancakes since I was right all along."

"Oh no, you don't!"

A BROKEN WINDOW

"Justice isn't something that you can just proclaim. It's a feeling you should keep near your heart."

– Miwako Sato, 'Detective Conan'
(Roychoudhury, 2021, para. 23)

It was a lovely afternoon. Basel had just left his house, ready to enjoy the warm sun while playing on the swings in the park.

He was just going to turn around the corner when Basel saw a frustrated Mrs. Parker cleaning her front patio. Shards of broken glass clinked together as Mrs. Parker swept them across the floor and into a dustpan. They sang the tragic story of a beautiful patio being ruined.

"Mrs. Parker," Basel called out to the elderly woman muttering to herself angrily.

Mrs. Parker turned around, raising the broom in her hand like a sword as though ready for a duel. The expression on her face forced Basel to take a step back. If it had been possible, Mrs. Parker's eyes would have shot lasers at him right then and there.

"Oh, it's you, Basel dear," Mrs. Parker calmed down as soon as she realized who it was. The vengeful beast inside gave way to her normal angelic self.

"It's me," Basel smiled awkwardly. "But what happened to your window?" he asked hesitantly, pointing at the patio window.

"That happened!" Mrs. Parker's eyes flashed, pointing at something through the window.

Basel shifted from left to right, then stood on his tippy toes. Through the broken window, Basel saw a soccer ball lying inside Mrs. Parker's living room, with a cluster of glass shards all around it.

"Who did it?" Basel asked, understanding how someone had thrown or most likely kicked the ball right through the windowpane.

"Oh, I don't know!" Mrs. Parker said hopelessly, sitting down on one of the patio chairs.

"You really didn't see anyone?" Basel repeated.

"By the time I'd come out running, there was no one in the street." Mrs. Parker explained. "I only managed to catch a glimpse of two boys a few blocks away turning a corner, both of the same height and with blond hair."

"Hmm..." Basel tapped his chin, and looking around, Basel coincidently caught eyes with Mrs. Hill from across the street, who quickly closed the blinds. Mrs. Hill did not like kids or other people, for that matter.

There was no use in knocking on her door to ask if she had seen anything.

“That’s all I have.” Mrs. Parker sighed.

“Something is better than nothing,” Basel reassured the distressed woman. “Let’s see where that ball can lead us first.”

Basel left Mrs. Parker to her cleaning and ran to the soccer field. It was near the park, and the town’s soccer team practiced there a few times a week. Basel looked down at his watch and saw it was almost four in the afternoon.

“They should still be there!” Basel muttered to himself and quickened his speed.

***

Huffing and puffing, Basel breathed a sigh of relief when he reached the soccer field and saw that the team was still there. He swept his eyes across the field seeing many blond heads.

Jake and Brian, best friends with similar heights, and the Coleman twins, Harry and Mark. “It has to be one of these kids, but which of them could it be?" Basel whispered to himself.

PHWEEET!!!

The coach blew the whistle signaling it was time to practice penalty shots.

He watched Jake and Brian walk in front of the goal and line up. Jake placed a new soccer ball at his feet and got ready to take the penalty. It was clear from the way he stood that he had the goal in the bag. He casually blew a stray strand of wheat-colored hair from his forehead, then kicked the ball.

In the next second, the ball zipped past the goalkeeper and struck the back of the net. Jake simply smirked at his teammates, who stood to the side clapping for him, and then turned around to face his best friend.

"You can do it, Brian!" Jake yelled as he gave him a thumbs up.

Compared to Jake, Brian was much more somber. Fingering his fair-colored hair, he took a deep breath. As soon as the coach blew the whistle, Brian delivered a strong kick. However, he ended up being off-target.

The ball zoomed over the goal, not even managing to touch the front goalpost.

Harry and Mark Coleman shot similar shots as Brian, not even getting close.

The coach then divided the boys into two teams and told them to get ready for a practice match. Basel didn't stay much longer. It was getting late.

***

The next day when Basel met up with Mrs. Parker, she finally had something more solid to share.

"This came in the mail today," Mrs. Parker said, slapping a piece of paper on the table in front of Basel.

"What is it?" He asked curiously as he leaned forward to pick up the paper.

"See for yourself," Mrs. Parker shrugged.

The paper was entirely blank except for a single note written right in the middle. Smirking, Basel looked across the street and caught Mrs. Hill looking again as she quickly closed her blind.

"*? about the window.*"

"What does this mean?" Basel asked in confusion.

"Your guess is as good as mine." Mrs. Parker said.

"My goodness, that's it!" Basel suddenly stood up. "I know who broke your window."

What do you think the note means? Who broke Mrs. Parker's window? The clues are all in there, so make sure you read carefully.

If you think you've cracked the case, go to the solution on the next page.

SOLUTION

A BROKEN WINDOW

"Who?" Mrs. Parker asked, moving forward in her seat.

"It was clear from my visit to the soccer field that the kid we were looking for was either Jake and Brian or one of the Coleman twins," Basel explained. "They were the only pair of blond boys of the same height there."

"But they're all such nice boys," Mrs. Parker insisted.

"That's the thing," Basel said. "They must not have intended to break your window. It must have been an accident after which they ran away."

"But who did it?" Mrs. Parker asked.

"The note is quite clear," Basel smiled. "Question *Mark* about the window"

"Mark Coleman?" Mrs. Parker gasped. "That can't be. There's no other proof."

"But there is," Basel said. "When I went to see their practice yesterday, the twins took really bad penalty shots, just like Brian. They were way off target. There's no way Jake could have broken the window because he looked so confident just before he scored the goal. Mark is a blond twin, and with the help of a certain friend..." Basel looking across the street, "... you know who to *question*."

Mrs. Parker sighed, "So, it's Mark Coleman who I need to have a talk with, it seems."

Basel nodded, "Yup!"

WHERE IS SAM?

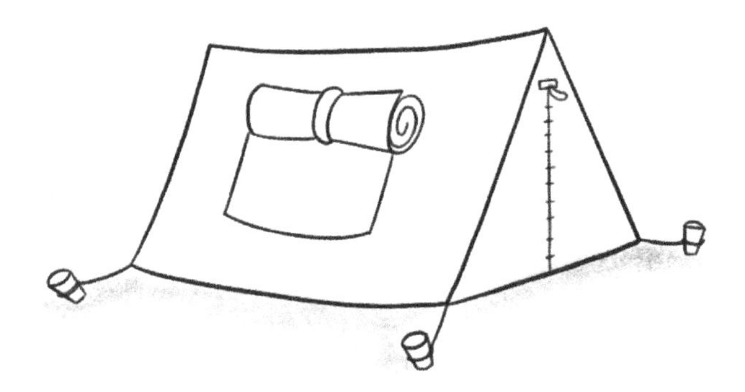

"Unless you are good at guessing, it is not much use being a detective."

Agatha Christie. (Quotelyfe, 2023)

Basel dribbled his soccer ball for a few minutes, then gave up and sat down on the grass.

"Where are you Sam?" He muttered in frustration as he glanced at his watch.

It was a bright and sunny Saturday morning, and just like mostly every week, Basel was waiting for his neighborhood friend in his backyard so they could play some soccer together. Basel had been out there for about an hour, yet still no sign of Sam anywhere.

This was very unusual of him because Sam was never late before. Actually, Sam loved coming over and playing soccer so much he would usually arrive even before Basel was ready. Although, he did sometimes have medical appointments, Boy Scouts, or drawing classes he attended. But Sam would usually tell Basel about it.

It was getting hot, so Basel decided it was best to stop. Sam clearly wasn't going to come. Afterwards, Basel gave in to his curiosity and passed by Sam's house.

He ran up to Sam's door and rang the bell. A few seconds later, he came face to face with a very stressed-out Mrs. Muller, his mother.

"Oh…," Mrs. Muller said rather disappointedly.

"Hi Mrs. Muller, everything okay?" Basel asked curiously.

"Sorry honey," Mrs. Muller apologized. "I thought you were Sam."

Basel asked in confusion, "Is Sam not home? He certainly didn't come over to my house."

That's when Mrs. Muller rolled her eyes "Oh no, I wonder what he's gotten into now. He has a dentist's appointment in 30 minutes."

***

"Where do you think he is?" Basel asked.

"Thinking about it now, he was with his Aunt Ruth in the Kitchen earlier. He had been insisting for quite some time now to transfer to a new school," Mr. Muller explained from where he sat on the sofa with his wife.

"We never took it seriously," Mrs. Muller said. "He's studying in the best school in town. Why would he want to transfer somewhere else? He may be checking out the campus with Aunt Ruth, who has been more encouraging of the idea."

“We’ve called her but seems like her phone is off” Mrs. Muller said as she looked at the different sketches made by Sam that she had framed. There was one of a pine tree and another of a giant oak native to a forest nearby. Each is more amazing than the one before. Sam was famous in their neighborhood for his remarkable sketching skills, given how young he was.

“Do you mind if I take a look in his room?” Basel asked.

Mr. Muller nodded, “Sure. Follow me.”

Basel trailed behind Sam’s father as he went up the stairs and entered the first room on the right. Sam’s room was messier than Basel’s. Clothes covered almost the entire floor. One wall was covered with many of Sam’s own drawings.

He looked down only to find Sam’s school paperwork and letters lying on the table. Curiosity got the best of him, and he looked around the papers for any leads. Fortunately, there was a month-old open letter that read:

“...We apologize for the error in the shipment of your order. Your second tent in the color black will be sent to you in the next three days....”

"Ah! here it is." Mr. Muller shrieked. Basel immediately jumped away from Sam's laptop. He didn't want to seem like he was going through his son's things, "I was looking for this watch for weeks, must have left it in here while tucking him in one day," Mr. Muller muttered.

He turned to face Sam's dad and saw him standing in front of Sam's closet. Despite how many clothes were lying around, it seemed that Sam still had just as many in his closet and not a tent in site. The closet was divided into two sections. The upper one held his clothes, and the lower one contained his shoes. However, one pair was clearly missing. In its place was a shoe print created out of dried mud.

"He took his boots with him," Mr. Muller explained as he traced Basel's gaze to the closet.

Basel yelled, "Mr. Muller, I think I know where Sam is!"

How do you think Basel figured out Sam's location? Have you got any idea where Sam could be? All the clues you need to solve this case are in the story, so read carefully.

Don't turn the page until you think you've cracked the case! The solution is on the next page.

SOLUTION

WHERE IS SAM?

"Where?" Mr. Muller asked.

"He's in the woods!" Basel declared.

"In the woods?" Mr. Muller repeated doubtfully. "But how can you be so sure."

"Ask Mrs. Muller to call the Boy Scouts patrol leader."

Both went running down stairs to ask Mrs. Muller.

"Yes, that does sound right, Aunt Ruth usually takes him since she lives on the way. I'll call" Mrs. Muller said

"My suspicion was confirmed when I saw the crusted mud footprints in his shoe rack. Clearly, Sam took his muddy boy scout boots." Basel explained.

“He got a letter from a camping store informing him that his tent is on the way. There was no tent in his room, this means Sam must have taken the tent with him to boy scouts because they were learning how to set it up today!”

Mrs. Muller was getting off the phone, ” you were right Basel, he’s in the woods finishing up setting up the tent I’m going to pick him up now. We can still make his dentist appointment.”

“I never thought about all of this,” Mr. Muller muttered in awe. “My goodness Basel, what a little detective you came out to be!”

“He’s my friend too you know, he must have forgotten to let me know about our soccer meet up” Basel said. “Go get him and tell him we’ll play soccer next weekend. I missed playing with him way too much today.”

DECEPTION AT ITS FINEST

*"The criminal is a creative artist;
detectives are just critics."*

Hannu Rajaniemi (Quotelyfe, 2023)

Ding, Dong! Ding, Dong!

"Uncle's here!" Basel yelled excitedly as he ran to open the door.

Basel loved his mother's brother, not only because he was a very cool police officer but also because every time he came over, he would have some interesting case on hand too. He'd always allow Basel and Misty to help him with it.

"Uncle Mike, do you have a case you're working on?" Basel excitedly asked his uncle once dessert was served.

"I actually do," he said. "Well, not me, but it's something my friend discussed with me the other day.

"Can you share the details with us?" Misty asked as she dug into her cinnamon roll.

"Well… you know the rules," Mike said, shrugging his shoulders.

"We promise to not let a single word leave this room!" Basel vowed, and Misty nodded at his words. They both pulled their best puppy dog impression, knowing he could never resist it.

Mike laughed at their cute faces, "Okay, okay!" he raised his hands, giving up. "Well, there is a case in which I might need your help."

The kids immediately moved forward in their seats, eager to hear more.

"A husband and wife, Mr. and Mrs. Easley, returned to their apartment from work late at night since they each work an hour away from town, and saw that the wife's most precious vase had been stolen. The vase was actually an antique that was worth about one hundred thousand dollars." Mike explained.

"One hundred thousand dollars…." Misty eyes almost popped right out of her face.

"What else did the thief take?" Basel asked.

"Nothing," Mike replied.

"Well, if someone had a vase worth a hundred thousand dollars, they wouldn't need to take anything else," Misty said, still half-lost in how much the vase was worth.

"The apartment door was closed, I'm assuming, so how did the thief leave?" Basel asked.

"You're right. The door was closed," Mike answered as he scraped the last bit of cinnamon roll from his plate. "The husband and wife said that they opened the window and found a rope hanging out. The thief must have left through the window."

Before Misty or Basel could ask anything else, Mike's phone buzzed. It turned out he was needed at the police station and ended up leaving earlier.

Basel and Misty, on the other hand, had been intrigued by the case. They thought over the different possibilities before going to bed. The next day they were so excited to share their thoughts with Mike and see if there were any new developments, so the two of them decided to go see him at work after school.

"Who do you suspect?" Mike asked the kids as he added some important-looking papers to a file on his desk.

"The neighbors or a common street thief," They both said together.

“Did they even have any neighbors?” Misty asked, second-guessing herself a little.

“You’re lucky because they did.” Mike smiled. “The apartment building just opened three weeks ago, so it was just Mr. and Mrs. Easley and a kindergarten teacher living there. But why suspect the neighbor?”

“Well, apartments usually have the same layout, so the neighbor would be familiar with it,” Misty explained.

“And it would be easy for a neighbor to sneak in and out,” Basel added.

“Hmmm…” Mike muttered, seemingly mulling over their words. “Mysteries aren’t always easy, but that’s why we love them, don’t we?”

Knock! Knock! Knock!

“May I enter?” An officer, almost the same age as Mike, came in after knocking on his door.

“Ah, Jason,” A welcoming smile unfurled on Mike’s face. “Come, come.” He waved the officer in. Mike then pointed towards Misty and Basel in turn, “Meet my niece and nephew, Misty and Basel.”

Jason shook hands with both of them enthusiastically, “So, these are the little detectives you were telling me about.”

Mike beamed at the kids warmly, “Yup! They’re helping me solve the vase theft.”

“Well, if that’s the case, I’ve got something for you guys,” Jason said excitedly. “I talked to the teacher who lives under the husband and wife.”

“What did she have to say?” Mike asked.

“You know how there aren’t any security cameras installed in the apartment because it’s still new, right?” Jason inquired, to which Mike nodded. “So, I asked the teacher if she had seen any movement around her neighbor’s house that day.”

“She said she had been sick that day, so she took a day off from teaching at the school. Other than her mother, who came to visit her, she saw Mr. Easley coming home around lunch time with some food to eat. She had seen him when she walked her mother out.”

“Oh, my, that’s it!” Basel suddenly cried out. “I know who the thief is.”

What do you think? Who is the thief? All the clues are in the case. Make sure you read carefully to find all the clues.

If you think you've cracked the case, go to the solution on the next page.

SOLUTION

DECEPTION AT ITS FINEST

"The neighbor wasn't the thief," Basel said excitedly. "It's the husband, Mr. Easley!"

Jason and Mike simply nodded with a smile on their faces.

"It always bothered me what you told us when you came over for dinner." Basel continued, "you said the husband and wife claimed the thief left through the window because when they opened it, they found a rope hanging there. But the window should still have been *open* If the thief really did leave from there. This means someone hung the rope just to give off the impression that the thief had escaped from there and, by force of habit, *closed* the window."

"Correct!" Mike cheered.

"The neighbor told you that she had seen the husband return around lunch," Basel continued. "But the husband and wife both claimed that they had come home late at night and that they work an hour away. A little inconvenient for Mr. Easley."

"And...?" Jason prompted him for more.

"Uncle Mike, do you remember how Misty had said that if a thief had a vase that was worth a hundred thousand dollars, they wouldn't need to take anything else?" Basel asked, and Mike nodded in return. "Well, that statement caught my attention. An ordinary thief would most likely not have recognized on sight that the vase was that precious. He would have chosen to steal other things of value from the apartment. However, nothing else had been stolen from the house. It could thus have only been the Mr. Easley who knew how valuable the vase was and decided to have it all from himself."

"You're a genius, young man!" Jason praised Basel, making the latter blush.

"But wait a minute," Misty said. "you guys have already solved the case, haven't you." The two officers smiled smugly and nodded at her words. "And that paper was a copy of the original one, wasn't it?"

"Your niece is equally smart," Jason told Mike.

"Well, I'm a proud uncle." He said, looking at both the kids with shining eyes.

THE HAUNTED ROOM

"Crime is common. Logic is rare."

Arthur Conan Doyle, 'The Adventure Of The Copper Beeches' (Roychoudhury, 2021, para. 8)

Just like any other Sunday, Basel was waiting for his friend Sam in the neighborhood park so they could play ball. Things had been a little rough between the two friends since Basel had ruined Sam's escape plan by figuring out where he was hiding. Yet, it was behind them now. The two friends were back to being just that – friends.

"Basel! BASEELLLLLL!"

Basel turned around to see Sam running in his direction. A smile started to unfurl on Basel's face, but it quickly disappeared when he took in Sam's expressions. His face was as white as snow, and he breathed heavily as though he'd been running away from a ghost. A fine layer of sweat had gathered on his forehead.

"What's wrong?" Basel immediately asked in concern.

"It's a…a ghost!" Sam cried out.

Basel burst out into laughter at that, "What are you talking about?"

"I'm telling the truth; you have got to believe me!" Sam insisted. "My room's haunted!"

"How's that possible?" Basel muttered.

"I just saw it with my own eyes!" Sam said, "I knew Mom and Dad wouldn't believe me, and my sister would never let me live this down. So, I'm here to ask for your help."

"Well, then there's no need to wait any longer," Basel replied. "Let's go to your house."

The two of them went back to Sam's house. They were about to go up the stairs when they saw Mrs. Muller enter the hallway with a laundry basket in her hands.

"Hi, Basel!" Mrs. Muller Greeted.

"Hello, Mrs. Muller!" Basel replied with a smile.

"Oh, dear, I've told you before; please call me Ella," Sam's mom chastised. "Do stay for dinner though. I'm making casseroles."

Apparently, Ella was aware of Basel's weakness for casseroles. He simply couldn't say no to that. Basel nodded with a smile, then turned towards the stairs.

"Oh, Sam, before I forget," Ella stopped her son. "If you have any laundry, kindly hand it over. Sarah made a terrible mess of her shoes. I don't know where that girl is wandering around these days. Anyway, I'm doing the laundry, so if you have any dirty clothes, please give them. And ask Josh to do the same, please."

"Yeah, Yeah, Mom!" Sam replied distractedly.

We climbed up the stairs. Sam made a small stop at his brother's room, which had a Skull taped to its door, to relay their mother's message.

"Sorry about that," Sam said, a little embarrassed as he entered the room and closed the door behind him.

"Never mind," Basel said with a wave of his hand. "So, how did it all happen?"

"Well, I've been hearing some creepy, creaking noises at night for about a week." Sam began. "I first thought it was all Sarah's doing, but I just didn't find a speaker or anything of that sort."

"Today, while I was getting ready, the sounds started to come again. I had just changed my clothes when there it stood!" Sam pointed a shaky finger to the space between the window and his bed.

"What happened then?" Basel asked, walking to where Sam was pointing.

"I ran away as fast as I could," Sam recalled. "I'm just glad it didn't follow me."

Basel looked out the window and realized Sam's room wasn't that high up. The window looked out into Ella's vegetable garden. It was then that he noticed how the plants directly below the window had been crushed and, from there, spread out small indents as though someone tried to tip-toe out of there.

Before Basel could show these to Sam, his mom called them down for dinner.

Basel completely forgot about all the ghosts or the haunted room as soon as he stepped downstairs. The entire place smelled like heaven. Sam's mom, dad, and sister were already downstairs.

"Come boys," Sam's dad called from his seat at the dinner table.

"The casserole is almost done," Ella smiled from near the oven.

"Thank you for having me," Basel smiled. "Hi, Sarah!" He greeted Sam's sister as he took a seat.

"Hi," Sarah greeted back as she placed a pair of scissors in the drawer and dumped a few small pieces of white cloth in the bin.

Then Josh came listening to something through a skull-shaped earbud in his right ear, pinching Sam's arm for no reason other than to hear his younger brother scream. "Oww!, I'm going to get you back! " Sam responded irritated.

"Sarah, could you please come here and remove all your books from the table," Her dad said as he piled the books lying on the table to one side.

"But I don't have enough space in my room!" Sarah protested as she shifted the books from the table to the sofa in the living room.

"Darling, we've been over this before," Ella said as she took out the casserole from the oven and set it on the table. "Now, let's all enjoy this lovely dinner in peace."

Basel couldn't agree more. After dinner, The Muller family insisted that Basel stay for dessert too. As the children helped clear the table, Basel asked his friend a question. The answer was just as he had hoped.

"I think I know whose ghost has been haunting your room, Sam," Basel claimed with a smirk on his face.

Were you able to find out who's haunting Sam's room? The clues are all there, so be sure to read carefully!

Don't turn the page until you think you've cracked the case! The solution is on the next page.

SOLUTION

A HAUNTED ROOM

As Basel lay the dirty dinner dishes in the sink, he turned to face his friend, "Sam, has your sister been insisting on changing rooms?"

"Yeah," Sam said with surprise. "She's actually been wanting to get my room. Don't think she'll want it now that it's haunted though."

"Oh, no, she will," Basel said. "I think I know whose ghost has been haunting your room."

"Who is it?" Sam asked with curiosity. "Josh? Man, I knew it was him!"

"No, it's Sarah!" Basel claimed.

"But… how?" Sam asked.

“You remember how your mom complained about Sarah’s shoes being awfully dirty,” Basel said to which Sam nodded. “ Yeah, well, I saw the plants right under your window had been ruined as though someone had jumped right on top of them and then tried to tip-toe out of the garden as carefully as they could, especially if they knew someone in particular,” Basel pointed to Ella, “would be very angry with them if they found out.”

“You said how the ghost never followed you,” Basel continued. “So, the only way for a fake ghost to leave would be to escape through the window.”

“And when we came down for dinner, I saw Sarah handling some scissors and a few pieces of white cloth,” Basel said. “She would have those if she made a ghost costume by cutting out holes in a white sheet for her eyes.”

“In short, she’s the one who’s been haunting the room all along. She thought scaring you out of there was the only way for her to get what she wanted.” Basel concluded. “Even though it’s clear how much Josh likes messing with you and of how much of a fan he seems to be of the horror genre, he simply doesn’t have the motive to do this particular act.”

"Sarahhhh!!!" Sam cried out in frustration.

***

"You're grounded for an entire week," Mr. Muller declared after listening to the entire story. Ella nodded at her husband's words.

"There's just one thing I still don't understand," Sam said. "Where were all the creepy noises coming from."

Basel could see the pride on Sarah's face at Sam's question, but she immediately lowered her head when she saw her father staring at her. Josh, on the other hand, seemed to be impressed by Sarah's plan at that moment.

"I taped a Bluetooth speaker to the back of your cupboard." She muttered.

"I'll get you back for this," Sam swore darkly. "I'll get you back."

DAYTIME ROBBERY

"Crime is common. Logic is rare."

Arthur Conan Doyle, 'The Adventure of the Copper Beeches' (Roychoudhury, 2021, para. 25)

"I'll have a watermelon too," Basel's mom told the lady at the fruit stall.

"Mommmm," Misty whined in her most annoying voice, and she knew exactly which one it was. "Let's go to the sports aisle!" She insisted for the third time.

"Misty," Mom said through clenched teeth. She turned to smile at the lady packing their fruits as though to say, 'kids these days.' "Misty, you know the sports aisle is closed for the week." She warned Misty to get her act together.

Of course, Misty knew that. Basel knew she did. He also knew why she was doing this. Their mom had woken them up early in the morning, informing them that they were going grocery shopping. It would be less crowded and easier to shop.

There was no other way to convince their mom to leave but by force. And that force was *embarrassment*. Misty was doing everything short of throwing a tantrum (that would've been too much even for her) to try and force their mother to cut the trip short and go home.

Basel had tried his own set of things earlier, but nothing had worked so far. It was all on Misty now.

“Mommmm,” Misty continued her Oscar-worthy performance.

Ignoring her daughter’s antics, their mom turned to the lady, “Did you have that watermelon I asked for?”

The lady, who had probably been looking for the fruit under the table, looked up. “I swear there was one left from last night.” She partially muttered to herself.

“I’ll wait some more,” Their mom smiled politely.

Misty immediately turned to face Basel, “Do something!” She mouthed.

Together, the siblings were about to create some serious chaos when the fruit lady suddenly popped back up.

“It’s gone!” She cried out. “My Goodness, it’s gone!”

That instantly woke the kids up. They faced the lady with their full attention.

“What’s gone?” Basel asked.

“Someone stole the last watermelon!”

***

"When was the last time you saw the watermelon?" Misty asked.

"Right after the fight!" The lady said.

"Mrs....?" Basel asked.

"Mrs. Long," The lady answered.

"Mrs. Long," Basel nodded. "What fight?"

"Well, last night, two heavy-set men came. One had a green sweater, and one had a blue shirt," Mrs. Long began. "As fate would have it, both of them were about to have a baby, and their wives wanted to eat some watermelon. As you know, I only had one watermelon left. The two of them had caused such a huge fight I got sick and tired of them. I announced no one would get the watermelon."

"Were there any other customers at that time?" Basel inquired.

"Yes," Mrs. Long nodded. "Two other pretty fit women, who had just finished working out with loose clothes on, but I didn't sell it to them either. They did seem upset, now that I remember."

"Let's go see the recording!" Misty suggested printing to the security camera.

In the security footage, they saw the two men yelling at each other, with the one in the blue shirt yelling, "I'd settle it outside if it wasn't for my bad back!" and then Mrs. Long breaking them apart.

Both the men and the women behind them looked dejected at Mrs. Long's declaration and dispersed. Another camera showed how the blue-shirted man simply left the store and some 15 minutes later came back.

The footage then showed the two men continuing to circle the fruit stall after every 5 minutes, though it was difficult to tell what either of them was doing because of how crowded the place was. The cameras at the gate showed how the two women left 30 minutes later. One of them was pregnant and had only one bag in hand. The other had two bags. Then the green sweatered man left, he too was carrying one bag.

In the end, the man with the blue shirt had left as well, with a bag in one hand and the other holding a cotton soccer ball toy, though it seemed he was having trouble carrying it.

"But none of them had the watermelon…." Mrs. Long said in confusion.

But Basel simply smirked, "Oh, they did."

Who, in your opinion, stole the watermelon? The clues are all in the story, be sure to give it a good read to find the thief!

If you think you've cracked the case, go to the solution on the next page.

SOLUTION

DAYTIME ROBBERY

"Who?" The question was flung at Basel from four different places.

Basel looked at the confused faces of Misty, Mrs. Long, his mom, and the security guard.

"The two men continued to act suspiciously. After the fight, they now had a personal stake in getting the watermelon." Basel explained.

"And the way the blue-shirted man carried the soccer ball toy with difficulty had me thinking he must have stuffed the watermelon in the soccer ball toy cloth and carried it out of the store. It seemed the ball was much heavier than a normal one would have been. But then I realized what he had yelled to the man in the green sweater. He had a bad back anything he carried would made him struggle. Plus, he was already carrying another bag as well."

"So, who was it?" Basel's mom asked.

Basel asked Mrs. Long, "How did the two women look like to you again?"

"Fit women who just finished a workout with loose clothing," Mrs. Long answered.

"And how did they leave?" Basel asked

"One left pregnant!" The security guard yelled

"She put the watermelon in her shirt!" Misty said excitedly.

The store management later got in contact with the thief, and it turned out that much of what Basel had explained turned out to be true.

"Another case under the belt then?" Misty asked her brother with a smile.

Basel laughed, "You bet!"

THE CRISIS OF THE CACTUS

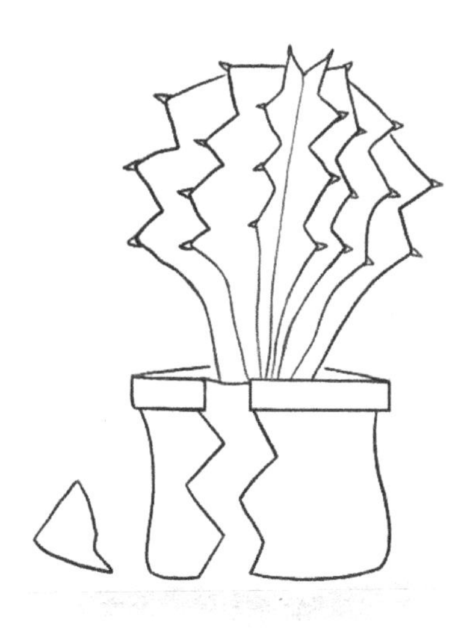

"Looks like we've got another mystery on our hands."

Fred Jones, 'Scooby Doo' (Roychoudhury, 2021, para. 19)

The entire class buzzed with excitement. Basel too wasn't immune to it. Their science teacher had promised to take them to the botanical garden on school campus.

The class had been divided into teams, and each team had been tasked to grow a certain type of plant. Basel and his team had grown a small plant that would become an apple tree in the future.

"Please form a straight line," Ms. Carla announced.

Quickly the entire class ran from their seats and tried to form the best possible line they could. Basel was the first one to get to the front of the class. Another boy, Kane, was there too, though he didn't seem quite happy. Poor Kane wanted to choose a different plant for this activity, but Ms. Carla didn't allow it. Apparently, he was still upset over it. Basel, however, didn't let anything ruin his mood. After a bit of pushing and pulling, the entire class was ready to leave.

Once they entered the garden, Ms. Carla showed each group the spot where they were supposed to seed their plant. It took half an hour for Basel and his team to finish the process under the instruction and guidance of one of the gardeners responsible for looking after the place. Ms. Carla took one last round of all the groups' performances and then asked them to line back up. Reluctantly, the students all got back into a single file, ready to go back to their class.

They were just about to leave when a gardener ran towards Ms. Carla. "Stop right there!"

"What's wrong?" Ms. Carla asked in concern.

"One of the cactus plant pots has been broken, "The gardener turned to look around at Basel and his classmates. "It was perfectly fine before your class came."

"That can't be...." Ms. Carla's faith in her class made Basel shake his head in disappointment. "Where is it?"

The gardener asked Ms. Carla to follow him, and the entire class decided to chase after Ms. Carla to learn more about this mystery. And where there's a mystery, there was no way that Basel would stay behind.

He was just about to run after his friends when he realized Nathan, a boy who was in Basel's group, remained where he stood.

"You aren't coming?" Basel asked.

Nathan looked up at him from where he was crumbling a piece of tissue paper, "No, I'm fine here. There's nothing interesting about a Cactus in crisis." Nathan muttered.

Basel narrowed his eyes, taking note of Nathan's red cheeks and nose. "Okay then." Shrugging his shoulders, Basel ran in the direction of where his class had gone. Though a sudden suspicion rose in Basel's mind, Nathan had disappeared for some time during their group activity, and no one knew where he had gone.

Reaching the crime sight, Basel pushed his fellow students aside to get to the front. There he saw the gardener showing Ms. Carla a huge Cactus plant that had been toppled over. The cherry-colored pot that the plant had been in was broken into three pieces while the poor cactus lay on the ground.

Ms. Carla looked furious, "Who did it?"

The entire class stayed quiet and looked down at their feet.

"Who was seen near this plant?" She asked in general.

For a minute, everyone stayed quiet. Then Kane came ahead. In order to reach the front with his huge figure, Kane pushed Basel aside and took his spot.

“Watch it!” Basel muttered, but it was as though Kane hadn’t heard a single thing.

“I saw Valerie standing next to it after she was done with her group project!” Kane pointed a pink-colored finger at Valerie.

The entire class gasped as they turned to look at Valerie, also known as the goody two shoes of the class.

“No, no,” I didn’t do anything. “I… was just there to admire it. I… I promise.” She stuttered. Flipping the sketchbook in her hand with her small hands, Valerie then showed Ms. Carla her drawing. “I was just making a sketch of it.”

Even though Ms. Carla had taken the sketch, it was clear from her expression how Valerie was still not off the hook.

Basel recounted the people he suspected behind this crime – Ms. Kane, the gardener, Nathan, Kane, and Valerie. It was then that it finally clicked for him.

"I know who did it!" Basel cried out.

Who do you think is responsible for damaging the cactus plant? How did Basel reach that conclusion? Make sure to read the story carefully to find out the actual culprit!

Don't turn the page until you think you've cracked the case! The solution is on the next page.

SOLUTION

THE CRISIS OF THE CACTUS

"Who is it?" Ms. Carla asked.

"I first thought it was Nathan." Basel began. "He went mysteriously missing during our group activity. And when I talked to him a few minutes ago, he wanted to stay away from the crime scene, and his face was deeply blushed as though he was embarrassed."

"That's ridiculous!" Nathan laughed. "I went to the bathroom because I have a pollen allergy. That's why I didn't want to come here and why my face was all red."

"I know," Basel said. "I assumed so when I saw the tissue in your hand."

"Let me just say also, it's not Valerie either," Basel said and saw how Valerie took a deep sigh of relief.

"How can you say that?" Kane asked with a frown.

"Firstly, it's clear that the cactus plant was a big one. Someone as small as Valerie couldn't have toppled it." Basel pointed out. "But we know someone who has the strength to do that," Basel said, looking directly at Kane's large frame.

He walked closer to the boy and raised his hand, palm up. "Kane's hands seem to be colored pink. They would have been as red as the cactus pot but to throw the blame off him, he clearly tried dusting them off."

"Last but not least," Basel continued. "We all remember how upset Kane was with Ms. Carla when she rejected his idea for the plant project. What other way to get back at her than by destroying a plant under her supervision and getting her in trouble with the principal?"

"Oh, fine," Kane stomped his foot. "Yes, I did it!"

Safe to say it was Kane who got into trouble with the principal in the end.

THE CASE CRACKERS

"Every man at the bottom of his heart believes that he is a born detective."

– John Buchan. (Roychoudhury, 2021, para. 11)

"Why did you have to reveal it!" Kane complained, waving his hands in the air.

Sam clapped him on the shoulder, "I asked the same thing from him!"

"Well. I'm glad he did," Valerie saluted Basel from where she sat on the bean bag near the window. "You practically threw me under the bus!"

"Ms. Carla would never have said anything to you!" Kane shot back. "She loves you, and now have an entire week of detention."

"Kids, kids," Grandma entered, a tray of freshly baked cookies and milk in her hand. "let's not fight."

"I'll help you," Misty immediately stood up from her window seat where she had been listening to the entertaining debate between Basel's friends.

"I can't believe I've already solved eight cases so far!" Basel praised himself. "I'm definitely the best detective in the world."

His claim made all the kids and Grandma fall into fits of laughter.

"What?" Basel frowned. "I solved the mysteries, didn't I!?"

"Yes dear," Grandma said. If Basel was being honest, it was still weird to hear Grandma call him "dear." How far indeed the two of them have come. "But just a handful of mysteries doesn't make anyone a world-class detective."

"It won't be just a handful of mysteries for long," Basel smirked.

"What do you mean?" Misty asked.

"I am going to launch my own detective agency!" Basel announced excitedly. "We'll solve mysteries not big enough for professional detectives like Uncle Mike to take up, but that are still important to the people of the community."

"Wait a minute," Valerie interrupted. "Did you just say *we*?"

"Of course, I can't do something this big without you guys," Basel smiled. Well… he did think he could, but it'll be much more fun to work with a team. "So, will you all join me?"

There was a minute of silence in which all his friends and Grandma looked at Basel in shock. And then they all erupted.

"OK!"

However, the only one who remained silent was Grandma. The kids turned to look at her with eager eyes.

"I'll join on only one condition," she said. "I get to be president!"

"The presidency can be yours if you can convince Mom to let us make our headquarters in the shed in our backyard." Basel negotiated, then put his hand out to Grandma.

Grandma immediately shook Basel's hand, "You have a deal."

"The only thing left now is a name…" Sam said, tapping his chin.

"I've already thought of it." Basel smiled. "The Case Crackers. There's not a case in the world that we can't crack!"

DETECTIVE MANUAL

Identifying Prints

The process of identifying prints is crucial, as no two individuals share the same fingerprints. Additionally, each finger on a person's hand bears a unique print, and it is important to distinguish which finger is being matched. Typically, prints from the index and middle fingers of the right hand are found more frequently. Thumbprints are the easiest prints to recognize, as the ridges flow up and away from the fingers. This applies to both the right and left thumbs.

Fingerprint patterns are of three categories:

- arches (plain arches and tented arches),
- loops (radial loops and ulnar loops), and
- whorls (plain whorls, double loop whorls, central pocket loop whorls, and accidental whorls).

In total, there are eight basic patterns, with loops comprising sixty percent of all prints and whorls making up 35 percent.

To match a print, begin by identifying which of the eight patterns it falls into using a diagram. Once the pattern is established, further analysis can be conducted. If a suspect's print does not match the basic pattern, they can be eliminated from the investigation.

When trying to match a suspect's prints to the basic pattern of a print, identifying unique identification points becomes crucial. Even the slightest difference between the two prints can eliminate the suspect.

Elimination fingerprints

Elimination prints are taken from a subject's hands and kept on record for future reference. To take elimination prints, an ink pad and a card with room for ten fingerprints and notations are required. The subject should wash their hands and relax their hand and arm muscles. The thumb should be rolled towards the body on the ink pad, and then immediately repeated on the print card. This process should be repeated with the remaining fingers of both hands. For palm prints, the subject's entire palm and fingers should be inked and pressed down on a separate card.

Hair and fiber analysis

Hair and fiber analysis may also be used in criminal investigations. Hairs and fibers left behind at crime scenes are often collected as evidence with the help of special vacuums.

The police use hair and fiber analysis to gather evidence at crime scenes, hoping to identify who has been there. While it is difficult to identify a specific person based on a hair or fiber, careful examination can lead to some deductions. To begin, examine the sample with a magnifying glass to determine whether it is a hair or fiber. Hairs get narrower from the shaft to the tip and have different textures than fibers. Placing several human hairs from different sources against a white background can help determine color, texture, curliness, length, and other characteristics. Similarly, fibers can be examined to narrow down the field of suspects. However, it is important to note that this type of evidence alone cannot make a positive identification.

Footprint evidence

Detectives can use footprints as evidence in investigations, but they don't always give a lot of information. If the footprint is from an athletic shoe and is clear, it can be easier to match to the brand, model, and size of the shoe. If the shoe is new, the pattern will likely have no wear or variation. But if there is a unique pattern, it can be matched to a specific suspect's shoe.

To get evidence from a footprint, you should take a picture of it first. Remove any debris around it and use a ruler to show the size. If you make a mistake while making a plaster cast, the picture can be used as evidence. Before taking a cast, make sure the print is not too wet.

If you can't wait for it to dry naturally, you can use a hair dryer. Be careful not to get the heat too close to the print, or it could be damaged. The print should be just dry enough to hold the plaster of Paris. Put a metal frame around the print to keep it in place while the plaster sets. Mix the plaster of Paris according to the instructions on the box.

Remember, plaster dries quickly, so work fast. If you can, use a rubber mixing bowl, since plaster won't stick to it. Otherwise, use any clean bowl that can be thrown away. Add plaster to the water until it has the thickness of pancake batter.

Begin by taking a continuous photograph of the footprint before casting it. It's important to remove any debris, like twigs and leaves, from the imprint before casting. Additionally, placing a ruler above or below the footprint can provide scale for the photograph. This photograph can serve as evidence in case of any errors during the casting process. Before starting to cast, make sure that the print isn't too wet, but also not too dry as it may flake or crumble. If it's too wet, a portable hair dryer can be used to speed up the drying process, but should not be held too close to the print.

To begin casting, place a metal frame around the print and press it gently into the soil to prevent it from expanding or changing shape during the casting process. Then, mix plaster of Paris according to the instructions on the box in a rubber mixing bowl or a clean disposable bowl. The plaster should be poured continuously, from one end of the footprint to the other, using a spoon or spatula to avoid damaging the impression.

After pouring the plaster, the cast should be reinforced with wire screening or green twigs to prevent it from breaking when it is removed. Once the plaster has hardened after approximately 30 minutes, remove the metal frame and gently lift the cast, taking care not to bend it. Allow it to dry for another 30 minutes and then use a soft-bristle brush to remove any soil from the bottom. The finished cast can now be compared to the suspect's shoes. It should have a thickness of 1 to 1.5 inches (2.5 to 4 cm) to provide an accurate comparison.

-The End-

THANK YOU

A thousand times thank you for purchasing my book!

There is always a risk in purchasing a book that might not suit you.

I could not be anymore grateful you had an opportunity to read all the stories in my book.

As a small favor I would like to ask you if you could please consider leaving a review on the platform? This would really humble independent authors like me a lot.

Any good feedback is very much appreciated and will help in the process of making more great short stories. Again, Thanks!

>> **Review Link Amazon US** <<

>> **Review Link Amazon UK** <<

REFERENCES

Goodreads. (2021) Arthur Conan Doyle > Quotes. Goodreads.com. https://kidadl.com/quotes/best-detective-quotes-for-budding-crime-fighters#:~:text=31%2B%20Best%20Detective%20Quotes%20For%20Budding%20Crime%20Fighters,creature%27s%20life%20is%20at%20stake.%E2%80%9D%20...%20More%20itemsreads.com)

PinkMonkey. (2019) Important Quotations - Quotes - The Hound Of The Baskervilles. PinkMonkey.com. https://kidadl.com/quotes/best-detective-quotes-for-budding-crime-fighters#:~:text=31%2B%20Best%20Detective%20Quotes%20For%20Budding%20Crime%20Fighters,creature%27s%20life%20is%20at%20stake.%E2%80%9D%20...%20More%20itemsBook Summary/Chapter Notes/Booknotes/Analysis/Synopsis/Essay/Book Report (pinkmonkey.com)

Quotelyfe. (2023) Agatha Christie Quotes. Quoteslyfe.com https://www.quoteslyfe.com/quote/Unless-you-are-good-at-guessing-it-339975.

Quotelyfe. (2023) Hannu Rajaniemi Quotes. Quoteslyfe.com. https://www.quoteslyfe.com/quote/The-criminal-is-a-creative-artist-detectives-634989.

Roychoudhury, R. (2021,March 13) 31+ Best Detective Quotes For Budding Crime Fighters. Kidadl.com. https://kidadl.com/quotes/best-detective-quotes-for-budding-crime-fighters#:~:text=31%2B%20Best%20Detective%20Quotes%20For%20Budding%20Crime%20Fighters,creature%27s%20life%20is%20at%20stake.%E2%80%9D%20...%20More%20items

Roychoudhury, R. (2021,March 13) 31+ Best Detective Quotes For Budding Crime Fighters. Kidadl.com. https://kidadl.com/quotes/best-detective-quotes-for-budding-crime-fighters#:~:text=31%2B%20Best%20Detective%20Quotes%20For%20Budding%20Crime%20Fighters,creature%27s%20life%20is%20at%20stake.%E2%80%9D%20...%20More%20items

Roychoudhury, R. (2021,March 13) 31+ Best Detective Quotes For Budding Crime Fighters. Kidadl.com. https://kidadl.com/quotes/best-detective-quotes-for-budding-crime-fighters#:~:text=31%2B%20Best%20Detective%20Quotes%20For%20Budding%20Crime%20Fighters,creature%27s%20life%20is%20at%20stake.%E2%80%9D%20...%20More%20items

Best%20Detective%20Quotes%20For%20Budding%20Crime%20Fighters,creature%27s%20life%20is%20at%20stake.%E2%80%9D%20...%20More%20items

Roychoudhury, R. (2021,March 13) 31+ Best Detective Quotes For Budding Crime Fighters. Kidadl.com. https://kidadl.com/quotes/best-detective-quotes-for-budding-crime-fighters#:~:text=31%2B%20Best%20Detective%20Quotes%20For%20Budding%20Crime%20Fighters,creature%27s%20life%20is%20at%20stake.%E2%80%9D%20...%20More%20items

Roychoudhury, R. (2021,March 13) 31+ Best Detective Quotes For Budding Crime Fighters. Kidadl.com. https://kidadl.com/quotes/best-detective-quotes-for-budding-crime-fighters#:~:text=31%2B%20Best%20Detective%20Quotes%20For%20Budding%20Crime%20Fighters,creature%27s%20life%20is%20at%20stake.%E2%80%9D%20...%20More%20items

Roychoudhury, R. (2021,March 13) 31+ Best Detective Quotes For Budding Crime Fighters. Kidadl.com. https://kidadl.com/quotes/best-detective-quotes-for-budding-crime-fighters#:~:text=31%2B%20Best%20Detective%20Quotes%20For%20Budding%20Crime%20Fighters,creature%27s%20life%20is%20at%20stake.%E2%80%9D%20...%20More%20items

Made in the USA
Las Vegas, NV
30 November 2024